RAIN MAKES APPLESAUCE
Appreciation by Jerry Pinkney

I first read *Rain Makes Applesauce* three years out of art school, shortly after designing and illustrating my first picture book, *The Adventures of Spider* by Joyce Cooper Arkhurst. The process of illustrating *Spider* captured my imagination in a way I had not expected and I was hooked. Bookmaking emerged as the new direction and focus of my career.

When I shared this with a fellow artist, he introduced me to four books that would change and shape how I pursued my vision of bookmaking until this very day: *The Wonder Clock*, written and illustrated by Howard Pyle; *The Wind in the Willows*, written by Kenneth Grahame and illustrated by Arthur Rackham; *The Honeybees*, written by Franklin Russell and illustrated by Colette Portal; and most importantly, *Rain Makes Applesauce*, written by Julian Scheer and illustrated by Marvin Bileck. I cherished these publications, fearing I might just wear out the pages.

Over the years, these books have taken their place on my shelves among other classics I have collected. However, it was Julian Scheer's delicious and poetic text and Marvin Bileck's stunning illustrations that I returned to time and time again for inspiration. Bileck's line, expressively nuanced, held so much power. His pastel palette added warmth to the overall feel of his vignettes. His art was rich in humor in the tradition of Pieter Bruegel the Elder's drawings and prints, and lyrical in the way of Carl Larsson's paintings. Bileck's art nourished and fed my own, acting as a high-water mark for what I desired to achieve in bookmaking. *It's not impossible for Marvin*, I'd think when I hit a roadblock and referred back to *Rain Makes Applesauce*. It is bookmaking at its best—an extraordinary knitting of text and art that stands the test of time.

To Susan, Scott, and Grey
and in memory of Leslie

Text copyright © 1964 by Julian Scheer • Art copyright © 1964 by Marvin Bileck
Introduction copyright © 2019 by Jerry Pinkney • All Rights Reserved
HOLIDAY HOUSE is registered in the U.S. Patent and Trademark Office.
Printed and bound in November 2021 at Toppan Leefung, Dongguan City, China
www.holidayhouse.com • First Edition
3 5 7 9 10 8 6 4 2

ISBN: 978-0-8234-0091-1 (hardcover)
ISBN: 978-0-8234-4361-1 (restored hardcover edition)

APPLE SAUCE

by

JULIAN SCHEER & MARVIN BILECK

Holiday House New York

The *stars* are made

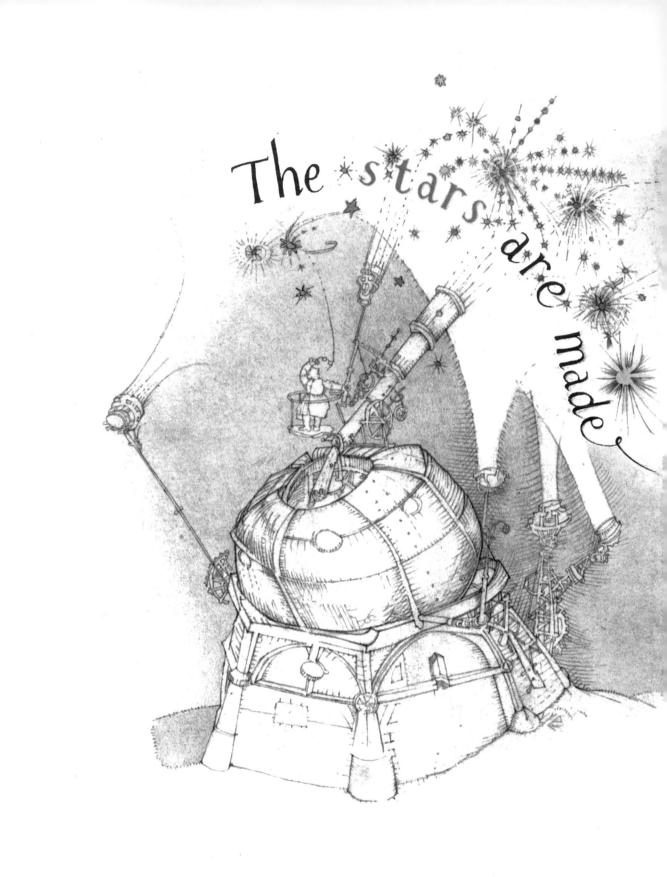

of lemon juice

and rain makes applesauce

oh you're just talking silly talk

I wear my shoes

inside out and rain makes applesauce

My house goes walking

every day

and
rain
makes
apples
sauce

Oh you're
just talking
silly talk

Dolls go dancing

on the moon and rain makes applesauce

The wind blows

backwards

all night

Monkeys mumble

in a jellybeanjungle

and

rain makes applesauce

Monkeys eat

the chimney smoke and

clouds hide in

Salmon slide

down a Hippo's hide

oh you're just talking silly talk

and rain makes applesauce

My Teddy Bear sings out

loud at night and rain makes applesauce

on a tickle tree

and

rain

makes applesauce

Oh, you're just talking silly, silly, silly talk.